My cat has eyes of sapphire blue,

J 821 FIS   02015321

Fisher, Aileen Lucia,
South Haven Mem Lib   26453

T5-DHH-673

MY CAT HAS EYES OF SAPPHIRE BLUE

SOUTH HAVEN MEMORIAL LIBRARY
SERVING: CITY AND TOWNSHIP
SOUTH HAVEN, MICH. 49090

MY CAT HAS EYES
OF SAPPHIRE BLUE

by Aileen Fisher

Pictures by Marie Angel

Thomas Y. Crowell Company · New York

Copyright © 1973 by Aileen Fisher
Illustrations copyright © 1973 by Marie Angel

All rights reserved. Except for use in a review, the reproduction or utilization of this work in any form or by any electronic, mechanical, or other means, now known or hereafter invented, including xerography, photocopying, and record- ing, and in any information storage and retrieval system is forbidden without the written permission of the publisher. Published simultaneously in Canada by Fitzhenry & Whiteside Limited, Toronto.

Manufactured in the United States of America

ISBN 0-690-56637-9
0-690-56638-7-(LB)

1 2 3 4 5 6 7 8 9 10

Library of Congress Cataloging in Publication Data
Fisher, Aileen Lucia,
        My cat has eyes of sapphire blue.
        SUMMARY: Twenty-four short poems about cats and
kittens.
        [1. Cats—Poetry] I. Angel, Marie, illus.
II. Title.
PZ8.3.F634Mv   811′ .5′2   72-13925
ISBN 0-690-56637-9
ISBN 0-690-56638-7 (lib. bdg.)

CONTENTS

1821

11-26-73

55004

To *Betsy, Honeybun,*
Quintus, Ben, Effie,
Timmy, and Priscilla

MY CAT

Her eyes at night
are ruby bright,
her day-eyes sapphire blue:

I think the sun
she traps by day
at night comes sparkling through.

CAT IN THE SNOW

Stepping gingerly,
he goes
through the garden
when it snows,
hoping not
to wet his toes.

And I'm sure
he never knows
every footprint
is a rose.

BOXES

My cat is fond
of cardboard boxes.
She plays she hides
from dogs and foxes.

She likes the box
with my old sweater,
but really likes
three boxes better.

ON GUARD

Sweep the floor,
but watch the broom!
A mini-tiger
stalks this room,
prepared to pounce,
to bring to doom
a monster vicious
as a broom.

WAGS AND PURRS

Dogs can wag
their tails like mad,

But cats can *tell* you
when they're glad.

5

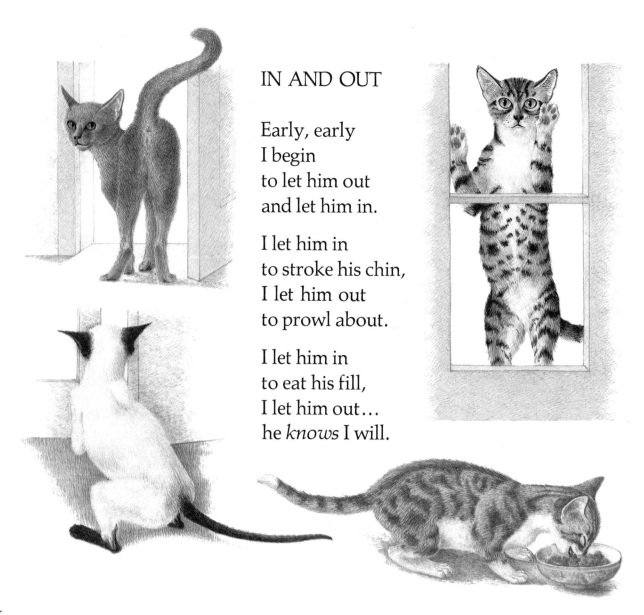

IN AND OUT

Early, early
I begin
to let him out
and let him in.

I let him in
to stroke his chin,
I let him out
to prowl about.

I let him in
to eat his fill,
I let him out…
he *knows* I will.

FUR OF CATS

Fur of cats,
it seems to me,
is wired with
electricity.

SUBSTITUTE

When Blackie
lost her kittens,
she sadly went to roam,

And found a baby rabbit
and carried it back home.

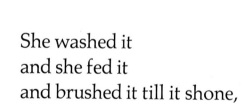

She washed it
and she fed it
and brushed it till it shone,

And burbled it a kitten-song
and raised it for her own.

HALF ASLEEP

To assume a cat's asleep
is a grave mistake.
He can close his eyes and keep
both his ears *awake*.

9

CAT BATH

She always tries
to look her best—
she washes east,
she washes west,
she washes north,
she washes south
with the washcloth
in her mouth.

And then, without
a sign of rush,
she makes her tongue
a comb and brush
to groom her fur
or, should she choose,
to smooth the velvet
of her shoes.

10

THE KITTENS

How limp they lie
all curled together,
as listless as
the August weather,
entwined in most
endearing poses
of arms and legs
and necks and noses…

It's hard to think
that on awaking
they'll be so fired
with mischief-making.

CAT WAYS

How calmly she sits
and stares at the scenery,

How lithely she flits
through thickets and greenery,

How deftly she hits
at a ball that is dear to her,

How fiercely she spits
when a dog comes too near to her.

12

YOUR CAT AND MINE

My cat has eyes
of sapphire blue.
Your cat has eyes of green.
My cat is of a
buffy hue,
and yours has tiger-sheen.
And you tell me,
and I tell you:
"*My* cat is better
through and through
than any cat I've seen."

13

GAME FOR AUTUMN

What's he waiting for,
I wonder,
near the maple,
halfway under?

What's he doing?
Oh, I know!
Waiting for a leaf to blow.
See him chase it!
See him go!

TOM

Thomas is quiet
all afternoon,
but sometimes he talks
rather loud to the moon.

CAT PLAY

Does she want
her rubber mouse?

Her ball that bounces
through the house?

That bit of harness
from the barn?

No! She much prefers
my yarn.

LISTENING

When it's time
for milk or fish,
my cat hears any sound
of Dish.

But when he's sunning
and I call,
he seldom hears
my voice at all.

17

CURVES

She sleeps a circle
on her mat,
my limber, yellow, curvy cat.

She curves an arc,
a bridge of fur,
by stretching up the height of her.

THE HUNTER

Patiently, how patiently
he crouches in the grass.

Does he see a telltale stir
and think a mouse will pass?

Staring eyes and tilted ears,
then whussssh! a cannonball…

Did you catch it, cat? Ho, ho,
a grasshopper, that's all!

POCKETS

Cats have secret pockets
in their padded paws
where, when they don't need them,
they can keep their claws.

ACROBAT

Did you ever
watch a cat,
the way he is an acrobat?

He twists his head
to reach a place
that seems too far to meet his face.

He puts his legs
at curious angles
as if to tie himself in tangles.

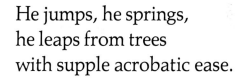

He jumps, he springs,
he leaps from trees
with supple acrobatic ease.

Then, vaulting lightly
to a shelf,
he makes a circle of himself.

KITTEN CAPERS

He plays with anything he finds
and then if that should fail
my kitten never really minds…
he always has
his tail.

KITTEN TALK

*Cat*tail,
*cat*nip,
downy little *cat*kin,
pussy-willow pussy
in a soft gray hatkin…

Do you know
they're named for *you*,
my furry little fatkin?

NEW KITTENS

Tibsy, oh, Tibsy,
oh, what did you do!
A nest full of kittens
all wiggly and new!
You're like the old woman
who lived in a shoe.

Six baby kittens
with thin squeaky voices…
which do you choose
(if a mother makes choices)?—
the striped, or the plain,
or the gray tinged with blue,
the white-foot, the patchy?
I'll give you a clue:

I choose *every one*
and I'll bet you do, too.

24

ABOUT THE AUTHOR

Aileen Fisher is America's most beloved writer of nature poems for children. She has written more than twenty books of verse, nearly all of them concerned with the birds, animals, insects, flowers, trees—and people—she knows and loves so well. Cats are her favorite animals, and her intimate knowledge of their endearing idiosyncracies is based on first-hand observation. Miss Fisher now lives in Boulder, Colorado, near the foot of the mountains she likes to climb.

ABOUT THE ARTIST

Marie Angel's meticulous miniature watercolor paintings of animals are eagerly sought by museums and private collectors in many parts of the world. Cats are her particular favorites, so it is natural that she should have enjoyed illustrating this book of Aileen Fisher's poems. Her pictures for a recently discovered manuscript by Beatrix Potter have won her accolades, as have her exquisite drawings for *The Twenty-Third Psalm*. Miss Angel lives in Sussex, England.